The
Nursery
Collection

Shirley Hughes

Lothrop, Lee & Shepard Books

New York

Copyright © 1985, 1986 by Shirley Hughes

First published in Great Britain by Walker Books Ltd., individually
as *Noisy*, *When We Went to the Park*, *Bathwater's Hot* (1985),
and *Colours* and *All Shapes and Sizes* (1986)

Printed in Italy

First U.S. edition 1 2 3 4 5 6 7 8 9 10

Library of Congress Cataloging in Publication Data
Hughes, Shirley.
The nursery collection / by Shirley Hughes
p.   cm.
"First published in Great Britain individually as Noisy, When we
went to the park, Bathwater's hot (1985), and Colours and
All shapes and sizes (1986) by Walker Books . . . London"—T.p. verso.
Contents: Bathwater's hot—When we went to the park—Colours—
All shapes and sizes—Noisy. ISBN 0-688-13583-8 (RTE)   1. Children's stories,
English.   [1. Stories in rhyme.]   I. Title.
PZ8.3.H8665Th   1993   93-47395
CIP   AC

Contents

 Bathwater's Hot

— 9 —

When We
Went to the Park

— 21 —

 Colors

— 31 —

All Shapes and Sizes

— 41 —

 Noisy

— 53 —

Bathwater's Hot

Bathwater's hot,

Seawater's cold.

Ginger's kittens are *very* young,

But Buster's getting old.

Some things
you can
throw away.

Some are nice to keep.

Here's someone
who is wide awake.

Shhh, he's fast asleep!

Some things are hard as stone.

Some are soft as cloud.

Whisper very
quietly.

Shout
OUT LOUD!

It's fun to run
very fast,

Or to be slow.

The red light
says "stop,"

And the green
light says "go."

It's kind to be helpful,

Unkind to tease.

It's rather rude to push and grab,

Polite to say "please."

Nighttime is dark.   Daytime is light.

The sun says
"good morning,"

And the moon
says "good night."

Good night !

When We Went
to the Park

When Grandpa and I put on our coats and went to the park...

We saw one black cat sitting on a wall,

Two big girls licking ice creams,

Three ladies chatting on a bench,

Four babies in buggies,

Five children playing in the sandpile,

Six runners running,

Seven dogs chasing one another,

Eight boys kicking a ball,

Nine ducks swimming on the pond,

Ten birds swooping
in the sky,

And so many leaves that
I couldn't count them all.

On the way back we saw
the black cat again.

Then we went home for supper.

Colors

Baby blues, navy blues,
Blue socks, blue shoes,

Blue plate, blue mug,
Blue flowers in a blue jug,

And fluffy white clouds floating by
In a great big beautiful bright blue sky.

Syrup dripping from a spoon,
Buttercups, a harvest moon,
Sun like honey on the floor,
Warm as the steps by our back door.

Scarlet leaves, bright berries,
Rosy apples, dark cherries,
And when the winter's day is done,
A fiery sky, a big red sun.

Tangerines and apricots,
Orange flowers in orange pots,
Orange glow on an orange mat,
Marmalade toast and a marmalade cat.

Berries in the bramble patch.

Pick them (but mind the thorns don't scratch)!

Purple blossom, pale and dark,

Spreading with springtime in the park.

Green lettuce, green peas,
Green shade from green trees,
And grass as far as you can see,
Like green waves in a green sea.

Shiny boots, a witch's hat,
Black cloak, black cat,
Black crows cawing high,
Winter trees against the sky.

Thistledown like white fluff,
Dandelion clocks to puff,
White snowflakes whirling down,
Covering gardens, roofs and town.

All Shapes and Sizes

Boxes have flat sides.
Balls are round.

High is
far up in
the sky.

Low is
near the
ground.

Some of us are rather short.
Some are tall.

Some pets are large. Some are small.

Our cat's very fat.   Next door's is thin.

Big Teddy's out.   Little Teddy's in.

Squeeze through narrow spaces.

Run through wide.

Climb up the ladder.

Slip down the slide.

Get behind to push.

Get in front
to pull.

This
jar's
empty.

Now
it's
full.

Hats can be
many sizes.

So can feet.

Children of all ages playing in the street.

I can stand up
very straight,

Or I can
bend.

Here's a beginning,

And this is the end!

Noisy

Noisy noises! Pan lids clashing,

Dog barking, plate smashing,

Telephone ringing, baby bawling,
Midnight cats caterwauling.

Door slamming,
Airplane zooming,

Vacuum cleaner
Vroom-vroom-
vrooming.

And if I dance
and sing a tune,
Baby joins in
with a saucepan
and spoon.

Gentle noises: dry leaves swishing,
Falling rain, splashing, splishing,

Rustling trees, hardly stirring,

Lazy cat softly purring.

Story's over,
Bedtime's come,

Crooning baby
Sucks his thumb.

All quiet, not a peep –
Everyone is fast asleep.